# Chrysanthemum Peg in Fairyland

Nancy Hardwick Turner

AuthorHouse™
1663 Liberty Drive
Bloomington, IN 47403
www.authorhouse.com
Phone: 1 (800) 839-8640

Published by AuthorHouse 06/28/2019

ISBN: 978-1-7283-1676-5 (sc)
ISBN: 978-1-7283-1677-2 (e)

Library of Congress Control Number: 2019908346

Print information available on the last page.

authorHOUSE®

# CHRYSANTHEMUM PEG IN FAIRYLAND

By Nancy Hardwick Turner

FAIRYLAND MAP

> NORTH TO TYELAND

CHURCH OF CHALK ROCK

MAMBY & PAMBY
THE SILLY SISTERS

PETAL ROADS
THE ROADS SCHOLAR

GARDEN OF THYME

THE CHERUBS
CHEMMA & CHEERLIE

THE ENTOMOLOGIST ROLL

TABUNT & TABOOSE
THE TALLEST GNOMES
IN THE WORLD

KITTENS

TREE OF KNOWLEDGE

DORBELLE THE WATCHDOG

MIX D. FROSTER, THE GREETER GNOME
CHRYSANTHEMUM PEG

GOLDFISH ROCK

< SOUTH TO THE GULL COAST & MARLARK'S HOME

EAST ENTRANCE TO FAIRYLAND

Chrysanthemum Peg in Fairyland
By Nancy Hardwick Turner

You may have tangible wealth untold;
Caskets of jewels and coffers of gold.
Richer than I you can never be—
I had a mother who read to me.
-from The Reading Mother by Strickland Gilliam

In memory of my mother, Elva Elizabeth Pegel Hardwick, who read to me and let my imagination soar.

Marlow, my mini me.

# Prologue

Amelia had thought long and hard about the petite pink piggy's uncomfortable situation. Generations ago, rumors flew that a boy named Smelliott had nibbled off one of the pig's legs thinking it would taste like bacon. It did not.

Smelliot seen sneaking in the succulents.

The pig needed a nice home, but didn't have a leg to stand on. Life on three legs can prove difficult at times.

Amelia pondered how to help the petite porker that she called Chrysanthemum Peg. Chrysanthemum because small pigs should have big names. Peg for German ancestors named Pegel and because Peg nearly sounds like pig.

Making a difficult decision, Amelia finally decided to take Chrysanthemum Peg to a hoof specialist and see if there was a possible prosthetic procedure for the unfortunately shortened limb.

# Chapter One

# Surgery

Pink pig prepared for procedure.

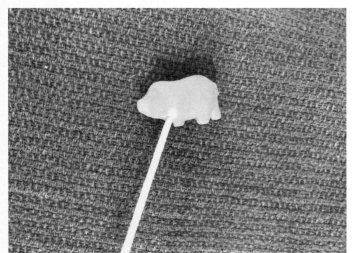

Procedure.

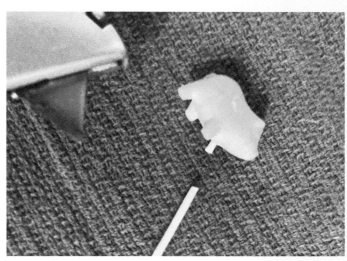

Prosthetician applies perfect pink paint to prosthetic.

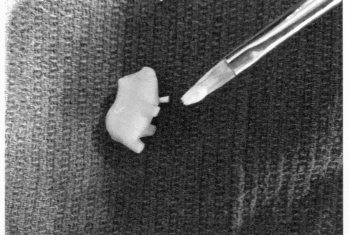

Recovery.

# Chapter Two

# Amelia Says Goodbye

**Chrysanthemum Peg hoofing around on her new leg**

Chrysanthemum Peg recovered quickly from surgery and was able to hoof around on all fours in no time. Amelia had researched homes for pigs and after speaking to some clever gnomes, determined that a certain Fairyland was just the place for Chrysanthemum Peg to begin a new adventure. The gnomes seemed well educated and education was important to Amelia. She was sure Piggy would have opportunities to learn in Fairyland.

And, so it was, with tears in her eyes, Amelia's gentle hands set Miss Peg into the welcoming arms of a somewhat preoccupied, yet kind, young gnome.

# Chapter Three

# The Greeter Gnome

The Greeter Gnome dropped what he was doing the minute Chrysanthemum Peg entered Fairyland. He had been raking, sweeping, and tidying up a somewhat run down mushroom cottage in anticipation of the new guest. He seemed a bit flustered, or frustrated, and appeared to be trying to do too many things at once. He was so busy and mixed up that he failed to introduce himself to the pig. Chrysanthemum was a little bothered by this lack of decorum because, after all, his title included the word greeter. He was friendly enough though.

The flustered gnome pointed Chrysanthemum to the road and they set out so the pig could become acquainted with her surroundings. She mentioned that there was a slight fishy odor upon entry. Gnome stated, "Some fool buried a goldfish nearby. It smells like a pig pen by that big rock." He instantly regretted his remark knowing it might have hurt Piggy's feelings. They hustled on past Goldfish Rock and went to meet the others.

# Chapter Four

# Chrysanthemum Learns a Gnome's Name

The Greeter Gnome waddled briskly down the lane with the tiny Chrysanthemum Peg hurrying by his side trying to keep up. Her three hooves and one peg made a very distinct and loud clip-clop-clip-tip-clip-clop-clip-tap which was not quiet at all on the brick path. Gnome's loud waddle-whoosh was equally as loud.

The two travelers came upon a soundly sleeping dog named Dorbelle by the side of the road. The hound was snoring loudly and never even looked up or heard the pair. "Some watchdog", thought Miss Peg to herself. She would have liked to meet a kindred spirit that walked on four feet, too.

Next, gnome and pig saw two adorable kittens who were busy biting bugs in a basket. They were so intent on tormenting the bugs that they never noticed when the polite pig prepared a curtsy. "I guess those two will have to get by on looks alone, because they certainly don't have very good manners." said Miss Chrysanthemum Peg to Mr. Unnamed Gnome.

When she said that, the gnome responded in a startled fashion, blushed, and immediately bowed and introduced himself as Mix D. Froster, named by his uncles, Tabunt and Taboose.

Piggy hoped that she would soon meet some residents with more sense than those met so far.

# Chapter Five

# The Entomologist

Chrysanthemum Peg and Mix D. Froster walked along until they stopped to meet a lovely young fairy who was holding a butterfly with its wings out like the pages of a book. "At last", thought the pig, "someone with brains." The cute pixie looked up and they all exchanged names. The fairy's name was Roll. She claimed to be an entomolologist who studied insects like her father before her. Her dad, she bragged, had named her after the Roly Poly research project he had done for his doctoral degree. He had studied possible medicinal uses for the pill bug. Chrysanthemum was very impressed by this interesting career.

Peg remarked to Roll that she liked the butterfly she was studying. Roll laughed and told her that it was a book about butterflies, not an actual butterfly. At that moment, the two page book fluttered its pages a little, perhaps trying to get out of the researcher's grip. Chrysanthemum noted to herself that she had never seen a book with only two pages that appeared to be trying to fly away. She decided that Roll had a lot to learn about books, bugs, and butterflies.

Chrysanthemum changed the subject and asked Roll where her father lived. Roll excitedly reported that he was doing research at the Gull Coast, near cousin Marlark, a spritely little coastal fairy. When piggy tried to correct Roll and asked if she meant the Gulf Coast, Roll haughtily said, "If I had meant Gulf Coast, I would have said Gulf Coast. They live at the Gull Coast and fly around with sea gulls all day." The pig had never heard of such a thing, but Roll claimed to be a budding scientist, so maybe she was right.

Chrysanthemum Peg made a mental note to ask her hoof specialist if she knew a wing specialist that could make some prosthetic wings for her so she could go fly with Marlark at the Gull Coast. She had always heard the saying "when pigs fly". She wondered, "When do pigs fly? And, how? And, where?"

# Chapter Six

# The Tallest Gnomes in the World

Mix and Chrysanthemum trotted down the road until they got to a lovely old cottage kept by Mix's uncles, Tabunt and Taboose. The uncles were the tallest gnomes Piggy had ever seen. They dwarfed Mix. They were friendly, but more interested in their garden and reminiscing about old thymes. Peg wanted to hear about their memories and old times, and she told them so. The uncles then recalled what a great herb crop they had last year, especially last year's rosemary and the old thyme.

In the middle of their reverie, the uncles suddenly realized there was planting to be done, as they were about to run out of thyme. They also questioned Mix as to why he had ventured so far from his sentry duties. They admonished him and instructed him to get back to Fairyland entrance, get the mushroom cottage ready for the pig, and told Piggy it was obvious why they named him Mix D. Froster. He was frequently mixed up, flustered, or frustrated!

Mix scuttled away before Chrysanthemum could properly thank him. He had been kind and friendly more than flustered and frustrated. She felt a little sad, but the older gnomes clearly knew best. Miss Peg felt abandoned, but the gnomes assured her they had a very educated fairy who would help continue the tour.

She heard a slow galumphing behind her and there came the cutest cherubic little fairy that Peg had ever seen. She was riding on the back of a slow moving frog. Tabunt and Taboose proudly introduced Chrysanthemum Peg to Petal Roads.

# Chapter Seven

# The Roads Scholar

Petal Roads was dressed smartly with soft pink flower petals splayed out on her head like a hat. Chrysanthemum admired the hat but Petal corrected her stating it was a mortarboard she received for graduating as a Roads Scholar. The petite pig inquired what it took to get to be a Roads Scholar. The little cherub informed her that she qualified for the title due to being on the road a lot riding her turtle. Miss Peg pointed out that the turtle was in fact a frog. The green fellow rolled his big eyes and Petal stated that he was a soft-shelled turtle.

Chrysanthemum declined to argue the point further because Petal was a smart scholar. The turtle winked, gave a little hop, and said, "Ribit."

On her green amphibian or reptile, Petal proceeded down the path with a sort of lumbering hop-hop. Chrysanthemum Peg clip-clop-clip-tipped with slight difficulty right along beside them. She was glad the pace was slow because she was so little and her hooves were getting tired.

Up ahead the trio heard cackling giggles and moved right along to see what was next.

# Chapter Eight

# Two Silly Sisters

Petal and Peg came around a bend in the path and there posed two of the prettiest pixies they had ever seen. They were giggling as they preened, applied fairy dust, and snapped selfies with their phones. The flighty fairies finally stopped their foolishness and introduced themselves.

Mamby and Pamby were two silly sisters, obsessed with phones. Chrysanthemum told them her name and they both exclaimed that they could never spell such a long name. They began to type into their smart phones and try spell check as they added Chrysanthemum Peg to their contacts. Finally, they placed her name as C. Peg because predictive text kept changing her name to Christmas Pug. The pig suggested that they should put down their phones and check a dictionary. Both sisters just gave blank stares. Soon Mamby said that perhaps they could get a dictionary from that bookworm, Roll. Pamby reminded Mamby that all Roll's books were about butterflies. After that, the fickle fairies resumed their phone fun, unphased by the fine idea of looking up words in an actual dictionary.

Chrysanthemum was glad to ramble on down the road with the scholarly Petal Roads. She was thankful the sisters hadn't relegated her to the spam file, a fear for all pigs.

Petal might not seem to be the brightest lightning bug in Fairyland, but she valued education like Piggy. It was a shame that Mamby and Pamby spent so much time on nonsensical tasks. She made a mental note to share a book with the silly sisters if their paths ever crossed again.

# Chapter Nine

# The Foreign Pilgrims

Clip-clop-clip-tip, clip-clop-clip-tap, lumber-hop, lumber-hop. On down the road the tour group went until Petal decided they should stop and chat with some cheerful chums that were hiking along the road.

The golden skinned cherubic chums carried backpacks. They chattered their names as Chemma and Cheerlie and were cheerful and charming. Chrysanthemum inquired about their interesting hike and from whence they came. Chemma chuckled and chortled that they were on a pilgrimage to the Church of Chalk Rock. Cheerlie chimed in that a kindly Mr. Do had brought them all the way from Tyeland for this quest. The swine had not heard of this foreign land, but she was familiar with many Asian lands and she planned to look up this place. Maybe it was near Viet Nam or Thailand.

While Chemma wanted to chat, she had to excuse herself to chase Cheerlie on down the road for he cheered that he could see the church in the distance. Petal Roads and Chrysanthemum Peg were interested in this opportunity to learn from the little pilgrims but Piggy was terribly tired. They could learn about the Church of Chalk Rock later.

Petal put the pedal to the metal and off they zipped at a snail's pace toward their destination, which was the mushroom cottage Mix had prepared for the sweet swine.

# Chapter Ten

# Best of Thymes

Shortly, the red roofed cottage came into view. Mix D. Froster was proudly waving, smiling and acting the part of a perfect greeter gnome. He had the mushroom cottage sparkling and smelling sweetly of fresh herbs, including the best thyme from the uncles' garden. He offered the weary wanderers refreshments, but Petal wanted to get home before dark. Chrysanthemum could barely keep her eyes open as she thanked Petal and her green steed and waved them on their way.

Mix helped the sleepy pig crawl into the lovely mushroom cottage. Before her little head even hit the pillow, her eyes were fluttering shut. She was a bit hungry, so right before she drifted off into gentle dreams, she rolled over and nibbled the cottage wall which tasted of toasted toadstool and chocolate truffle.

Fairyland was full of fascinating fairies and the four footed Chrysanthemum Peg would be well rested and ready for new opportunities to learn at sunrise. For that moment though, what was heard was, "Snuggle- snuffle- truffle- snack- smack- snort- snore. ZZZZZzzzzzzzzzzzz."

# About the Author

Nancy Hardwick Turner is a school nurse from Dallas, TX. The mother of three became an empty nester when her last child went off to college. The family pet of many years, a chicken named Puck Puck, moved to the great coop in the sky. Even the pet goldfish passed on.

Turner found herself with a big empty play fort containing a big empty chicken coop. With a love of gardening, she filled the coop with plants, decorative stones, and gradually a few gnomes and fairies. When a grandniece gave her a differently-abled little pig for the garden, the school nurse knew she could help the three legged hoofer be more mobile. The story of Chrysanthemum Peg began.

9 781728 316765